Christmas Shorts

Sylvia Mintz

BookLocker
Trenton, Georgia

Paperback ISBN: 979-8-88531-254-7
Hardcover ISBN: 979-8-88531-255-4
Ebook ISBN: 979-8-88531-256-1

Published by BookLocker.com, Inc., Trenton, Georgia.

Printed on acid-free paper.

The characters and events in this book are fictitious. Any similarity to real persons, living or dead, is coincidental and not intended by the author.

BookLocker.com, Inc.
2022

First Edition

Library of Congress Cataloguing in Publication Data
Mintz, Sylvia
Christmas Shorts by Sylvia Mintz
Library of Congress Control Number: 2022911485

Table of Contents

The Christmas Shack

Haven jerked awake as the car hit a pothole. She sat up straight and stretched. Checking out her new surroundings, she noticed the landscape had turned into a winter wonderland. She rubbed her eyes and looked over at Dylan.

Dylan had one hand on the steering wheel and the other around his mega-sized coffee cup. "Good morning, sleepyhead. Merry Christmas Eve."

"Whose bright idea was it again to leave at three in the morning?" She yawned and turned her head, looking in all directions. "Wow. Just a few hours, and we really are in the boonies, huh? The snow-covered trees are beautiful though."

"Yeah, we are making great time. A few more hours of nothing, and we will be at the very *center* of nothing, otherwise known as the Angel Farm. I bet Mom and Dad have been wrapping presents, baking cookies, and stringing Christmas lights all week. Not that they don't already have enough lights, gifts, and cookies. They are so excited."

He reached over and patted Haven on her thigh. "Thanks for agreeing to come. I know the whole country farm ain't your *thang.*" He glanced back at their three sleeping children. "But the kids will be stoked! They are so excited too. Gabriel just knows I have Cousin Eddie as kin."

Haven rolled her eyes. "If I have to suffer through watching *Christmas Vacation* one more time! The lines are already stuck in my head like a bad song you keep singing."

Dylan laughed. "And as soon as he is awake, he'll be playing that DVD for the rest of the trip."

An hour later, Dylan pulled into Delbert's Gas and Go. The kids slowly got out of the car and made their way inside to use the restroom. Haven waited for them at the cash register. "Go grab a snack if you need one," she said when they came out. "We are not going to be passing any Taco Bells or Burger Kings the rest of the way, so get something now."

The older man at the register nodded. "Nope, don't have any fancy eating joints around here. Have to drive an hour and a half just to buy a good pair of brogans."

Walking back to the car, Michael looked up at his mom and asked, "What's brogans?"

Haven smiled. "It's a kind of a heavy work boot." She shivered and looked around at the falling snow. "But what we need today are snow boots!"

She was glad they were going to have an old-fashioned country Christmas, and it was true that the kids could not be more excited. The boys were twelve and fourteen, still young enough to be interested in Dylan's stories. He had filled their heads with images of sledding down steep slopes, driving the tractor on the back forty, roasting chestnuts, making s'mores in the back yard, and being able to look into the night sky to try and pick out the Christmas star. You can't see many stars in the city lights.

Dylan was just finishing fueling up and cleaning the windshield when they started piling in. The car was covered with salt and grime from the road. He took a rag from the pump and made one swift swipe along the bumper to uncover angel wings. He winked at Haven before running into the store for his own bathroom break.

She looked at the angel wings and smiled. They'd had the sticker made specially since their last name was Angel. The kids loved the idea. They had named their two boys Michael and Gabriel, after angels in the Bible, and their daughter was Sera, for

Seraphim. She really was their little cherub. She was four and the sweetest of the bunch.

*

A bag full of snacks, numerous Christmas carols, and sixty miles later, the car began making an odd noise. The Check Engine light began to blink. Dylan patted the dashboard. "No, no, no. Come on, Bessie, don't act up now. Just another couple hours to go, ole girl."

A few more engine shudders, and it was clear Bessie wasn't going to go much farther. Their first chance to pull over was a dirt drive that didn't look well used, but it was better than the side of the road where snowplows had done their job scraping and piling snow. The car slid as they turned in, and they bumped into a small cedar.

Dylan put the car in park the car. It sputtered one last time and the engine went silent. He popped the hood and got out to check the car and their surroundings. Gabriel and Michael unstrapped their seatbelts to join him. "You boys bundle up," Haven called out as they shut the car door. "It's freezing out there!"

After a few seconds, Dylan tapped on the car window. "Hey, the boys and I see a cabin up the hill. We are going to go see if they can help us out." She nodded and they disappeared through the snow, which had started coming down heavier now.

The car hood was still up, so Haven couldn't see the cabin or anything else. She unbuckled her seatbelt and told Sera to crawl up there with her.

Sera wedged between the two front seats and snuggled up with her mom, waiting for the boys to return. With her head resting on Haven's shoulder, she asked. "Why did Daddy call the car Bessie?"

Haven smiled. "That's just what men do, sweetie. They name things."

After a few minutes, the boys returned. Dylan opened the car door and told Haven and Sera to climb out on the driver's side, since their side was in the ditch. The boys were dragging a small sled by a pull rope. Dylan popped the trunk and loaded the cooler onto the sled.

Haven stared at him; eyes wide. "What are you doing? What's wrong with the car? Did you find someone to help?"

Dylan laughed. "Let's see. First, unloading the cooler because those bellies will be empty soon. Second, the car is dead, and I am not a mechanic, so I don't know. And lastly, no one is in the house.

It looks abandoned, but it does have electricity. So, until we get help, we are setting up there. It's too cold to stay in the car."

Haven glanced at the cabin and plopped Sera on her hip. "Tell me you're joking."

"Nope." Dylan slammed the trunk. "Look at it as an adventure."

The boys began pulling the sled up the hill. Michael looked over his shoulder at his mom. "This place is so cool!"

Sera clapped. "It's a 'venture, Mommy!"

Haven stared at the exterior. "Not that it isn't totally abandoned looking, but are you sure no one lives here?"

"Well, the steps were piled high with snow. We are the ones that shoveled it off. Door was unlocked. No food to speak of in the fridge, and it is dusty, musty, and smelly inside. Probably a hunting cabin. Big game territory around here. Like I said, the power is on, and so is the water." Seeing her pained expression, he eased her up the steps. "Come on, babe. We need to get the kids out of the cold."

The inside of the cabin was…brown. Everything was dusty and dull. What lighting it had wasn't enough to make it bright or happy. Sera jumped down and ran to investigate her new surroundings. Haven took her cell phone out of her bag, but there was no signal.

Dylan shook his head. "I don't have a signal either. Probably in a dead zone. Landline is dead too."

"Seriously, in this day and age, who doesn't have cell service? I know your parents don't have a cell phone, but that's by choice. Right?"

"I promised you a technology-free holiday." He wrapped his arms around her waist. "Look, there is some firewood around the side of the house. Me and the boys are going to get a fire going in the fireplace. Heat is set low, and systems looks pretty outdated. I don't think we should tinker with it too much."

Haven raised her eyebrows and pushed his arms away. "You sound like we are setting up camp, Dylan. What are we going to do to get out of here?"

"Look, let us get a fire going to heat this place up, and then we will figure it out. I can't think when I'm cold. Don't worry, babe. We will get some help." He kissed her on the cheek and started toward the door. Grabbing the handle, he turned toward her and winked. "We got this."

Sera twirled around in the middle of the room. "It's a 'venture, Mommy!"

Haven went to the window. Dust flew when she pulled back the curtain. She had to rub a spot clean with her glove to be able to see outside. The boys were loading wood in their arms, laughing like it was any other day. Laughing! All she could think about was crying.

When the fire was going strong, Dylan stood up and turned to see Haven. Her arms were folded across her chest, eyes never leaving Dylan's. He indicated that they should sit at the table.

Turning his chair away from the kids, he whispered, "Look, babe, I'm sorry. This stinks, I know." He glanced around the room. "Literally. But I saw a hardware store a couple miles back. It was open, but being Christmas Eve, they may not be open all day. I am going to hike back there and see if they know a local mechanic. I should be able to call Dad. We'll figure something out."

Haven started to speak, but Dylan squeezed her hand tighter. "Look, I know you don't want me to leave, but I can't do a thing here. The kids think this is an adventure. Don't get all worked up. OK? It's Christmas Eve. I know this is bad, but let's don't make it tragic. Things happen for a reason." He put his hand under her chin and lifted her face to his. "Please, babe. You are a strong woman and a great mom. You can do this. Besides, if you freak out, they freak out. Either way, I am still heading to that store."

A tear rolled down Haven's face. She wiped it away, nodded, and sat up straight. "You're right. I can do this. *We* can do this."

Dylan gave her a hug. "I promise—no matter what, I'll be back before dark." He clapped his hands. "OK kids, huddle up."

The boys sat Indian style on the floor in front of him. He picked Sera up and plopped her on his knee. "Here's the deal. No cell service here because we're in the boonies!" He laughed and tickled Sera in the side, making her laugh. "So, here's the plan: I am going to walk up the road a little bit and see if I can get Ole Bessie some help."

Gabriel sat up on his knees. "Oh, oh. Can I go too?"

"Sorry, bud. I need you here." Dylan nodded toward the front door. "I want you and Gabriel to sweep the rest of that snow off the front porch, and then I want firewood stacked beside the door waist-high. Bring some in here too and fill up that wood box over there. Keep watch on the fire and add wood whenever you see it getting low. Just like we do when we go camping."

He nodded toward Haven. "Now, when you get done with that, you check in with your mama. We've got to make this place spick and span. I don't know who uses this place, but we are mighty grateful to use it today, and what is our motto when we borrow something?"

Both boys smiled. "Always take it back looking and working better than when you took it."

"That's right! So, let's clean up this place and leave some old hunter a nice surprise." Dylan turned back to Haven. "I checked the oven, and it works. Can't think of a better way to make it smell like home than to break open that roll of sugar cookies in the cooler. Might have to heat up those casseroles later if I don't get back soon."

Haven smiled. "Don't think I was so silly bringing all that food now, do you?"

"Things do happen for a reason, and God always provides. Sometimes he just provides a man with a smart wife." He slapped her knee and then stood up. "OK, troops, I'm heading out! Wish me luck—and when I get back, I expect to see some progress!"

Haven and the kids waved from the porch as Dylan headed down the driveway. When they couldn't see him anymore, the boys went toward the wood pile and their assigned duties.

Haven was surprised when she found a sudden burst of energy and actual excitement to spiff the little cabin up. She had always been a neat freak, and she found cleaning extremely therapeutic—and boy, did she need cleaning therapy now. The cabin didn't have much, so it didn't take long to make real progress. She took the rugs and curtains outside for a good dusting. She swept all the floors and even tackled the dirty windows. When the boys finished with the wood, they cleaned the two outside windows on the porch and knocked the cobwebs down from the ceiling, inside and out.

When they asked for their next assignment, Haven didn't know what to tell them to do. She realized the place was clean but not festive. It was getting later in the day, and she was concerned that spending the night there might become a reality. She snapped her fingers. "I have it, boys. Go back to the car and see if you can cut down that little cedar tree your dad hit. Take the axe, but please be careful. Also, look in the car and bring me my big blue bag. We're putting up a Christmas tree!"

The boys did as they were told and brought the little sapling to the porch. Haven found an old red metal bucket hanging by the door. They put the tree down in the bucket, placing rocks around the trunk to keep the tree upright and straight. When they brought it in the house, she went through her blue bag and pulled out five battery-operated Christmas bulb necklaces. She had bought one for each of them to wear for a Christmas Day selfie. They wrapped them around the tree and turned them on. It was beautiful.

Inspired by the tree, she found a metal coat hanger and stretched it out to form a circle. She sent the boys out in search of holly, red berries, and pinecones to make an old-fashioned wreath for the door. Sera loved to color and paste, so Haven had brought along a few craft items to keep her busy. She asked her to draw a pretty picture they could use somewhere in the room. When the boys returned with their woodland treasures, they made a beautiful wreath for the front door and added some glitter for effect.

All day as they worked, the kids laughed and enjoyed the busyness of their tasks. Haven had to admit it was the most quality time she had shared with them in weeks. There was a TV in the room, but the ancient rabbit-ears antenna could pick up only fuzzy local channels. It was nice to be without it.

However, while digging around in one of the cabinets, the boys found a DVD player that had never been opened. Michael begged to hook it up, and Gabriel ran out to the car to get his *Christmas Vacation* DVD. Haven turned toward Sera, who was sitting at the table, busy with her drawing. "And just like that, Ms. Sera, our ole fashioned country Christmas is over."

Sera laughed. "It's a 'venture, Mommy."

Dylan didn't see another car, so he had to walk the entire way to the hardware store. The distance turned out to be more like four miles than two, seeming especially far since the snow was coming down so hard. He checked his phone a couple of times. He was getting spotty service again, but now his battery was low.

The store was still open, he was happy to see. He walked in, shook the snow off his jacket, and stomped his boots on the rug. There were two men running the store. An elderly man sat behind the counter, and a tall, lanky teenager was working out front putting out stock. He was the one who greeted Dylan and asked how he could help. Dylan explained his car troubles and asked if he knew a mechanic he could call.

The young clerk shook his head. "Man, I don't know. Closest garage is in Rawlings. They close the week of Christmas, though. Old Man Phillips has a tow truck, but he's laid up now with the gout."

Dylan nodded and decided he'd better try to call his parents. He borrowed the store's phone and got through to his father. He told him about the car and said that if they couldn't get a mechanic or a rental, his dad would have to send help the next day. It was getting too late in the day for his parents to try to find them in the dark, especially with the heavy snow coming down.

With the store owner's help, Dylan spent the next two hours calling mechanics from other nearby towns, but all were closing early or not open at all. It was hopeless.

The older man looked at him sympathetically. "Look, young fella, I wish I could help. I really do. I don't know what to tell you, but you stay here as long as you need to. Go get your family and spend the night right here in the store if you need to. Nobody will bother you."

It's a Wonderful Life was playing on the little black and white TV behind the counter. Dylan nodded toward the screen. "Unless I get my own Clarence to show up and help me, I would appreciate a ride back to my car when you close up. I can't stay here, but I don't think I can walk all the way back in this weather."

The old man nodded. "Ain't too many angels available today, I guess, but we'll be happy to give you that ride."

The clerk nodded. "Just call me Yellow Cab. I've been giving Mr. Reynolds a lift every day this week."

Dylan walked outside and stared up at the sky. The snow fell like big feathers on his face. As frustrated and miserable as he felt, it was quiet and peaceful. Snow memories from his childhood came flooding back for a moment, and he felt calm.

His reverie broke when a loud oversized vehicle came sliding into the lot. He had never seen anything like it. The truck was a huge double cab with a snowplow attachment on the front and a wrecker attachment on the back.

A big burly man hopped out of the cab. He walked like a man with purpose, taking long strides. He had a plaid hat with fur-lined ear flaps. He paused mid-stride and looked at Dylan. "Hey, man, they still open?"

Dylan nodded.

The man slapped his thigh. "Blessed Jesus, Joseph, and Mary! Woohoo! I just knew I was too late. I got to get me some lead pipes to stick in the ground for my fireworks tonight and some..." He tilted his head and came closer to Dylan. "Dylan? Dylan Angel?"

A rush of recognition flooded through Dylan like adrenaline. "Billy Blakely?"

The brute nodded, wrapped both arms around Dylan, and lifted him off the ground in a bear hug. "I can't believe it!"

The clerk inside paused from his work. "Well, what do you know? Sounds like somebody just pulled in that knows that fella. Talk about Christmas miracles." He snickered. "Wonder if his name is Clarence."

Billy talked nonstop inside the store as he gathered what he called his Christmas Eve party supplies, slapping Dylan on the back every few minutes. His strange supply list didn't make much sense to anyone but Billy. However, it was probably the biggest sale the little hardware store had had all day. All week, in fact.

After he paid for his haul, the two men walked out. At the front door, Dylan hesitated and turned back toward the old man. "Thank you for letting me hang out here today. I hope you both have a Merry Christmas. Your little store has been a blessing to me today, so thank you."

The old man nodded, and Dylan ran out to catch up to Billy.

The clerk smiled. "How about that, Mr. Reynolds? Here we are minding our own business, and we wind up seeing a Christmas miracle."

Mr. Reynolds took out his handkerchief and wiped his nose. "Glad to see someone getting a miracle." He said it more to himself than his employee. The clerk started back sweeping whistling *Jingle Bells*. Outside, twilight was setting in.

At the cabin, Haven was now anxious. It was only five, but the sun had set, and Dylan had promised to be back before dark.

She turned the oven off. Their food was ready, and would hopefully stay warm until Dylan arrived. Haven examined the cabin and what they had done. It was truly unbelievable. Old quilts served as the tablecloth and coverings for the furniture. Fresh holly and cedar decorated the table and mantle, making the little room smell like Christmas. Mixed with the aroma of sugar cookies, sweet potato casserole, and honey-baked ham, it was inviting enough for Scrooge to enjoy.

Sera tugged at Haven's hand. "Mama, write our name on my picture."

Haven looked down at the paper Sera lifted toward her. "OK, baby, let me see what you did." It was of course a picture of five angels. She loved drawing angels. The boys had helped her sprinkle glitter and make some fancy swirls on the wings. Haven took her marker and across the bottom in big block letters wrote: THE ANGELS. Sera smiled and placed the card in the center of the table for decoration.

"Let's set the table, sweetie." Haven got out a dish and arranged the place setting at the end of the table, using a sprig of holly by the plate for decoration. "Now we need to make four more settings just like this. Want to help me?"

Before she had begun the second setting, lights flashed across the front of the cabin. The kids ran to the front window. The little cabin vibrated as a vehicle at the end of the drive let down a blade with a thud and began pushing the day's snowfall up the driveway toward the side yard. With one push, the driveway was clear, and all their footprints erased. With a beeping sound that would wake Rip Van Winkle, the truck began to back up toward old Bessie. Someone hopped out of the passenger side of the truck and waved toward the cabin. Sera clapped her hands. "Daddy!"

The boys stepped out on the porch. "Wow. That truck is awesome!"

Dylan was joined by the driver at the back of the truck. He pointed toward the cabin, yelling something to Dylan. Dylan nodded and ran to join his family on the porch. When he reached them, he was breathing heavily as he leaned down to kiss Haven on the cheek. "Sorry I'm late."

Haven reached up, wrapped her arms around his neck, and pulled him toward her. "I was worried sick."

Dylan pulled her arms down and held her hands close to his chest. "Figured as much. But it's all good." He nodded toward the wrecker/snowplow/truck. "Got a ride from an old friend."

As if being called, Billy bounded up the drive stomping on the bottom step with a thud. "Hear tell somebody here needs rescuing! But what I want to know is, who here likes fireworks?"

The boys both raised their hands.

Billy winked. "What about Christmas Eve midnight sledding and snowmobile racing?"

Both boys raised their hands again.

"Well, you better get a move on then. We got places to be and things to do. I'll go move some things around in the cab. Might be a tight squeeze, but she'll hold us. The car is already hooked up and ready to roll." Billy turned and strode back to his vehicle. His silhouette in the headlights gave him the appearance of Bigfoot.

Haven turned to Dylan. "Who is that, and where are we going? My gosh, Dylan, he looks like Cousin Eddie! Do you really know him?"

Dylan laughed. "He is an old friend. He lives an hour from here. Has a buddy that can look at Bessie for us tonight at his Christmas Eve shindig. If he can't fix it, Billy will drive us out to Mom and Dad's in the morning."

Haven looked doubtful. "Just please tell me he doesn't live in a camper."

"I don't think Billy would fit in a camper." He turned toward the boys. "What are you waiting for, guys? Go get your stuff. You heard the man. We got big plans tonight!"

They all headed back in the cabin. The boys grabbed their jackets and gloves. Gabriel was so full of excitement that he struggled to zip his jacket. Dylan reached down to help him. "Gosh, Dad, this is like the best Christmas *ever*!" When they were suited up, the boys practically jumped down the steps running toward the open door to the cab of the truck.

Haven squatted to put Sera's jacket on her. Dylan looked around the room. "Wow. This looks great. I am almost sad we can't stay here tonight."

Haven smiled. "Leaving it better than when we borrowed it, right?" Finished with Sera's jacket, she stood and put the stack of dishes they had never set out back in the cabinet.

Dylan came over and put his arms around her from the back. "Leave the rest, sweetie. We really do need to go. I'll grab the cooler. Just make sure everything is turned off and grab your stuff." He picked Sera up with one swoop and grabbed the cooler.

Sera giggled. "Are we still having a 'venture, Daddy?"

Dylan smiled. "Absolutely! Now, tell your mama to get a move on. She is slowing down the train!"

Dylan went out the door. Haven could hear Sera giggling. "Woooh-woooh! Mommy! We're going on a train."

Haven smiled and took one final look around the room. She turned off the lights but left the Christmas tree lights on. They were battery operated and would eventually burn out on their own. Grabbing her blue bag and glancing around for anything else of theirs, she sighed. "Goodbye, little Christmas cabin. Thanks for the 'venture."

Climbing in the cab of the truck was no easy feat. It sat a good three feet off the ground. Dylan helped Haven inside, pulling the door shut behind her. She plopped down on the few inches available on the seat. Everyone was already singing *Jingle Bells*, with Billy's voice being the loudest of the bunch. Billy backed the truck and Bessie out like a pro, and in minutes they were on the highway.

Haven gasped. "I left the food. You grabbed the cooler, but I had emptied everything into the fridge and had my casseroles warming in the oven."

Billy glanced up in the rearview mirror to meet Haven's eyes. "There won't be a shortage of food tonight. We will have a king's spread laid out in the barn." Looking at the boys seated next to him. "Tell me, fellas, has that city slicker dad of yours ever cooked you any good deer meat?" The boys shook their heads. Billy continued to run through every animal in the woods, acting appalled at their dietary shortages.

Haven looked at Dylan and whispered. "We're eating wild game in a barn?"

Dylan laughed and patted her thigh. "It's an adventure, babe, and a Christmas Eve I promise you will never forget."

Haven sighed and, though she knew they were long gone from the cabin, she looked back. It really had been a good day after all.

Mr. Reynolds locked the door on the little hardware store as his clerk pulled up on his truck and waited for his passenger. He felt tired in his bones, even more than usual. That stranger hanging around all day had taken something out of him that he couldn't explain. At first, he'd pitied the man when he'd seemed so lost. And then when his miracle happened, Mr. Reynolds had felt jealous. It wasn't like him to envy what other people had, but he had. Why couldn't he have a little miracle?

When Mr. Reynolds was settled in his seat, his driver pulled out of the lot. "Mr. Reynolds, my mama told me to invite you Christmas Eve dinner with us tonight. She's making oyster stew. It is kind of our tradition."

Mr. Reynolds shook his head. "I appreciate the invite, but I think I will pass."

"Well, what about tomorrow for lunch? We will have a crowd over, and the food will be enough for Pharaoh's army." He cleared his throat and shifted in his seat. "I, ah, I know this will be your first Christmas since your wife died and I, well, we all just thought maybe you would want to be around other people."

Mr. Reynolds gave him a sad smile. "I appreciate it. I really do. But I wouldn't be much company. Tell your mama thanks, and if she sees fit, you can bring me a slice of her pecan pie when we open back up after the holidays."

"You got it, Mr. Reynolds. I will hook you up nice."

When they got close to Mr. Reynolds' house, the first thing he noticed was the little cedar sapling that he was constantly brushing with his truck making the turn into his drive was gone.

"Well, would you look at that. Looks like Mr. Phillips finally came over and scraped your driveway. Maybe it's your Christmas present."

"Maybe, but unless he had some help, he couldn't have swept off my porch. Remember that big pile of snow that dropped off my roof onto the steps this morning? It's gone now, and my porch is loaded with firewood."

"Well, maybe it's your Christmas miracle, Mr. Reynolds."

Mr. Reynolds nodded and gingerly slid out of the truck looking around, still a little skeptical at his homecoming surprise. As he was closing the door, his driver lifted his hand. "Merry Christmas, Mr. Reynolds! See you on Thursday—with a whole pie, if I can hide one."

Mr. Reynolds nodded and made his way to the front door. He knew the clerk would wait until he was inside before he backed away. The door to his little cabin had a wreath made of fresh pine and stepping inside, he thought he was in the wrong house.

It smelled wonderful. There were hot coals in the fireplace still heating the room, waiting for another log to rev the flame back up. The table and mantel were decorated with greenery. Some of his wife's quilts were laid out, and in the corner of the room was a Christmas tree with little colored lights. The DVD player he had received last year from his clerk was set up beside his little TV on the cabinet, and the entire cabin had been cleaned.

He didn't know what to think. Who would have done all this? In the kitchen were more surprises. The oven had enough food for a week, warm and ready to eat. The refrigerator was packed with odd things he had never seen before—juice in little square cartons and cake balls on little plastic sticks.

The table was beautifully set for one. Mr. Reynolds collapsed in the chair at the end of the table. He looked up, blinking tears from his eyes. "Honey, did you do all this? Did you send me a Christmas miracle?" He took his handkerchief out and wiped his eyes and blew his nose. The last thing that caught his eye was the card placed on the table. THE ANGELS.

Later that night, any celestial viewer would have observed the Angel family enjoying all that Billy had promised. A buffet eaten in a barn, midnight sledding, snowmobile races, and fireworks. It would be a Christmas Eve like no other.

And anyone inclined to peep into the window of the little Christmas shack later that night would have observed Mr. Reynold sitting in his chair, a warm fire burning, eating a cake pop, and sipping from his very first juice box. An observer would also witness him watching *Christmas Vacation* all the way through...twice, laughing harder the second time around as he anticipated his favorite scenes.

There will always be enough Christmas miracles to go around to those that need them most, and you never know who your angels will be.

Little Faces

Shasta slipped her hood back on her head and looked up at the stormy sky. She glanced over at the gentleman ringing the Salvation Army bell. She hoped he remembered that she'd given a donation on the way in. She pushed her buggy as fast as she dared, almost trotting to the car.

The clouds were ready to burst—she could feel it. The wind was fierce, and the temperature was dropping. It felt colder now than it had when she'd entered the store thirty minutes ago. Approaching her vehicle, she hit the back hatch button on her remote. The door was slowing going up when she reached the back. Waiting for it fully open, she glanced over at the car beside her.

A lady was bent over unloading her bags into her trunk while trying to talk on her phone. Two little girls who couldn't have been more than four stood by the back door holding hands. The oldest one smiled at Shasta and gave her a little wave. Shasta smiled back and began unloading her own bags. By the time she had finished and pushed the buggy away, it was raining.

Shasta climbed in the car, relieved, and slammed the door. She threw her purse into the seat beside her and pulled out her phone. Three missed calls. She listened to the first message, which was from Russell, as she wiped raindrops off her face.

"Hey, babe. Be careful on the roads. Going to be slick, and those bridges could already be icy. I'll be home by noon and I, ah, I …got a call from Michelle at the adoption agency. I know you are not quite there yet, and I am not pushing, but let's talk when we get home. OK?"

Shasta let out a sigh. Poor Russell didn't know how to handle her ball of emotions. He was right: she wasn't there yet, but she knew, like he did, that she would be. It was their last option. Neither one wanted to move forward without being one hundred percent all in. Russell was just ahead of her. She would sit down tonight and tell him her real, selfish reasons for holding back. Maybe her confession would be enough to get her own heart fully on board.

As she pulled out of the crowded parking lot, the rain began coming down hard. Even with her wipers going full speed, everything was a blur. At the stoplight, she could see traffic was going to be a nightmare, so at the last second, she slipped into the other lane to turn left. She would go home the back way. It took longer, but there wouldn't be any traffic. She couldn't handle the chaos right now.

Stewart Road was quiet, and though Shasta was focused on the road, she let herself relax a little. Approaching Stewart Bridge, she reached down to grab her phone again. When she glanced down to locate it on the seat, the car hit a puddle. The familiar sound of water pounding on the undercarriage sent her hand instinctively back to the steering wheel. The car swerved to the left and although she didn't panic, she overcorrected the steering wheel.

The next few seconds passed in slow motion. Shasta watched the raindrops splatter on the windshield as if in a time-lapse film. Tree branches scraped along the side of the car, and it seemed as though she saw each pine needle as it swished by the window.

At first, there was no noise at all. Silence reigned as she felt the car being lifted. She was airborne.

It felt like minutes before the car's nose changed direction and began its downward motion. It was at that point when sound returned to her world. Splintering wood. Metal scraping against metal. As loud as those sounds were, she also picked up on grocery bags shifting, a can rolling on the floorboard, the contents of her purse being dumped and…

Giggles from the back seat.

Pain. Moans. It took her a several seconds to realize that the moans were coming from her. Her head pounded, her whole body ached, and she felt cold. Had she passed out? How long had it been?

She blinked several times, trying to erase the blurriness that clouded her vision, but everything still looked white. There was also a strange burnt smell. She realized the airbag was covering her face. She tried to move her right hand to remove the airbag, but pain shot through her like an electric shock. She closed her eyes again and gave in to oblivion.

Shasta slowly opened her eyes. This time, the air bag was gone. She could feel it tucked under her chin in a wadded-up mass. She couldn't remember doing that but was grateful to be able to see.

The windshield was busted; cracks large enough for pine branches to protrude into the car. She could smell the pine. Metal twisted all around her, and she realized that this was the biggest hinderance to her movement. She was pinned.

She tried each leg and arm slowly to see if she had wiggle room. There was none. Every body part she tried to shift was immediately halted by pain or some obstruction. Her head leaned against the window, and she was restricted in how she could move it, limiting her sight lines.

She heard water running, and the rain. Usually, the sound of gentle rain and a trickling stream were soothing. People bought sound machines just to have these noises lull them to sleep. But now these noises were frightening. Her feet felt wet. Fear gripped her. Was she in the creek? She gasped, but the movement sent such pain through her body that she felt herself slip back into darkness. Right before it went black and silent, she heard another sound that she remembered. Giggles.

This time when Shasta opened her eyes, she felt more determination. Her situation was not good. In fact, she was running out of time, and she knew it. She could sense that water had now passed her ankles and was up to her knees. It was still raining, and the creek was rising.

She tried once again to move and found it hopeless. She tried to calm her mind and think about how to help herself. She didn't know how long she had been trapped. Even if Russell had missed her at home, he would never expect her to have taken this route. Shasta closed her eyes and breathed a quick prayer. "Lord, help me. Please don't let it all end like this. I have—"

Shasta stopped mid-sentence. She heard whispers and again the giggle of a child.

Tentatively, Shasta whispered, "Hello? Is someone there?"

She heard rustling and then saw brown curls dangling in front of her. Next came a little button nose and chubby cheeks. Even as Shasta recoiled from the shock of seeing something so unexpected, she realized that the little girl looked oddly familiar. The child shifted around so she wasn't dangling upside down and slid into the passenger seat. Shasta realized it was one of the little girls from the parking lot.

"Oh, my goodness, sweetie. How did you get here? Are you OK?"

The little girl nodded. "We are fine, silly."

Shasta gasped. "We? Is your sister here too?"

The little girl smiled and nodded.

Shasta was panicked. "Why did you get in my car? Your mom will be frantic."

"No she won't. She wasn't even our mom."

Shasta remembered how the woman had been more interested in her bags and talking on the phone than in the two girls standing in the cold. Their coats didn't even look warm enough for this weather, and now they were trapped with her in a rising creek, and it was beginning to grow dark. She had a deep longing to give the girl a hug. "Are you sure you're not hurt? Can I see your little sister so I can be sure she is OK?"

The little girl reached over the seat. She tugged on the jacket of her little sister to gently drag her over until she was nestled beside her. Unlike her sister, her hair was straight, but she had the same big brown eyes and button nose. Her face was narrower with a paler complexion, like a China doll.

Shasta looked at the little girl and smiled. "Hello sweetie. You look OK. Do you hurt anywhere?"

The smaller sister whispered something in her older sister's ear.

The oldest sibling nodded. "Leah, wants to know if we can eat some of those oatmeal cookies you got at the store."

"Of course, you can. You two must be starving. You can have anything you want. I think there are some potato chips too."

The older girl reached over the seat and retrieved the box of oatmeal cookies. They both opened one up and began to eat. "Leah loves oatmeal cookies. They are her favorite."

Shasta smiled. "My husband's too. I have to buy a box every trip to the grocery store, so we don't run out." The older girl nodded and giggled. Leah must have the same addiction, she mused. "So, what's your name?"

Before the older girl could answer, Leah yelled, "Izzy!"

The older girl smiled and nodded. "That's what she calls me."

Shasta smiled. "Izzy? Does she mean Lizzy?"

The older girl nodded.

"I like that. You are a good big sister, I bet."

The girls helped themselves to more oatmeal cookies.

Shasta realized she needed to get help for herself—and now these girls. The water had crept up to her thigh. The creek was still rising. Then it hit her: she couldn't move, but they could!

"Hey, Lizzy. I need you to help me. I don't want you to hurt yourself and I know you might have to reach down in the cold water, but look around on the floor or the seat and see if you can find my phone anywhere."

The car was tilted, evidently lodged on something in the creek. The driver's side was deeper into the water than the passenger's side. The girls were still safely above water. Leah munched on her cookie and Lizzy began her search for Shasta's cellphone. After several whispered prayers, Shasta saw Lizzy's face light up when she held up the phone.

Shasta laughed out loud, which sent a jolt of pain through her body. But she was focused now. Pain couldn't stop her—she had to save these girls. "Good job. Now sweetie, I want you to help me call somebody, OK?" Her phone had been on silent, so even if someone had called her, she would not have heard it ring.

Shasta made hundreds of calls a week on her phone. By reflex alone, she knew what button to select to do her task. She could make a call without even looking at the device. But right now, she was trying to figure out how to explain to a child how to do the right steps to get a call to go through.

Then the phone lit up. Lizzy was holding the phone up facing her, so Shasta could see that it was Russell calling. "Lizzy!" Shasta shouted. "Hit the green button with your finger!"

Lizzy took her chubby little index finger and tapped the big green button on the screen.

Shasta started yelling. "Russell, it's me! I am on Stewart Road in the creek! I can't—" The car shifted in the current, and pain ripped through Shasta's body, once more taking her into darkness.

As her eyes closed for what she believed would be the last time, she saw Lizzy and Leah staring at her and then darkness.

Flashes of bright lights. Loud sounds of metal-on-metal grinding, causing vibrations that made Shasta grunt in pain.

Brown curls close to her face. Lizzy. She smiled at Shasta. "Thanks for the cookies. We have to go now." She bent down and kissed Shasta on the cheek and climbed over the seat. She reached down for Leah's hand and began to gently pull her over. Leah gave Shasta a smile and a wave before she disappeared into the back seat with her sister.

Bright lights. Too bright. Shasta blinked until her focus returned. Russell and her mother were standing at her bedside. She was in the hospital, and she was safe. Russell was holding her hand. He smiled down at her, worry and relief etched in his expression. "Hello there. You going to stay with us this time?"

Tears rolled down her mother's face as she let out a sigh. "Oh, thank God. Thank You."

A week passed, and the doctor sent Shasta home to recover. She had suffered a slight concussion in the accident, but miraculously had no broken bones. She had a total of thirty stitches in various locations on her body, and all her muscles still ached. Her bruises gradually took on every color in the rainbow.

She was healing physically, but mentally, she was a hot mess. When she'd come to in the hospital, she'd asked the staff about the two little girls in the car with her. At her insistence, the emergency team that had rescued her came to see her twice while she was in the hospital. They told her the same thing each time: there was no one else in the car with her. There couldn't have been. The car was crushed, and even if they had survived, there was no way they could've crawled out of the vehicle.

To appease her, Russell had called the sheriff's department and checked to make sure there were no missing girls in the area. A couple of off-duty officers had even offered to look in the surrounding woods and downstream. Nothing.

But Shasta couldn't let it go. She hadn't imagined those two precious girls. They were real. She had described the incident in the parking lot when she'd seen them even before the accident. Couldn't they check the security footage from that day? Russell suggested that maybe seeing those girls had made her dream them up after the blow to the head.

In another week, Christmas was upon them, so even though she wasn't convinced, Shasta decided to let it go. They gathered at Russell's parents' house on Christmas Eve. Shasta tried to join in the laughter and fun, but found herself walking around their home instead, looking over all the decorations and family photos.

Russell's mom went over the top with Christmas decorations. She included old family Christmas photos of Russell as child as part of her decor.

Shasta stopped abruptly when she came across one photo that she had never seen before. She grabbed the photo off the bookcase and ran to where Russell and his mom were exchanging stories at the kitchen island and drinking cocoa.

Shasta slapped the picture down on the bar. "Who is this? Who is this little girl?"

Russell and his mom looked at the photo and then both burst out laughing. His mom picked the picture up and smiled. "I found this last week. I thought I had lost it. This was always one of my favorites. It's not a little girl. It's Russell. He never did like to have his picture taken, but I snapped a good one this day, and he never even knew it."

Shasta gasped. "But that's her! That's the girl that was in the car with me. Lizzy. This looks exactly like Lizzy."

Russell gently reached for Shasta's hand. "Well, that's me, babe, and I'm pretty sure I wasn't in the car with you—and definitely not as my four-year-old self." He sighed and rubbed her hand. "You never told me the little girl's name. So, you think her name was Lizzy?"

Shasta pulled her hand away. "Don't look at me like that. I know what you are thinking. Lizzy. Short for Elizabeth. The name we had picked out for our child if she had been a girl." She wiped a tear from her face. "Russell, I am not crazy. Those girls were there. I didn't dream them up."

Russell sighed. "And there were two, right? The exact number of miscarriages you've had, babe. Don't you see? Even the name Lizzy. It all fits." He reached out and drew her in for a hug. "Don't torture yourself like this. Look, you took a nasty bump on the head, and we've been hit with some tough life events. Things are just jumbled up right now."

Shasta leaned into his shoulder and quietly sobbed. "But they were so real, Russell. And her name really was Lizzy." She turned and picked up his old photo. "And I swear she looked just like this." She smiled and gently rubbed her fingers across the little face in the photo. "But Leah. She was different. Hair straight as a stick and a slim face, but the same big brown eyes."

She turned back around to face Russell. His face was drained of color and his eyes wide. Shasta put the photo down. "What's wrong, Russell?"

He fumbled into his pocket and pulled out his wallet. His hands were shaking. He pulled out a folded piece of paper. "You said the other little girl's name was Leah?"

She nodded as Russell handed her the piece of lined notebook paper. It was two lists: boys' names and girls' names. *Elizabeth* took the top spot on the girl's list. They had agreed upon that a long time ago. But next on the list of girl's names was the name Leah.

Shasta looked at Russell. "What is this?"

Russell took the list back and stared down at the worn paper. "My list of baby names. Leah was my second choice for a little girl. That would have been the one I would have wanted if we had had two daughters. I never told you, for obvious reasons." He laid the paper down on the bar and looked back at Shasta. "I mean, what are the chances of that? You never even knew." A tear rolled down his face.

Russell's mom glanced at the list and put a hand to her mouth. She slipped out of the kitchen leaving the two alone.

Shasta reached out for him, and they embraced tightly, sobbing into each other's arms. Shasta was the first to break away. She looked up at Russell. "Do you want to know the real reason, the very selfish reason, I couldn't be one hundred percent on board with adoption and give up on having our own kids? Because we *did* have two. Not for very long, but we had two, and I daydream constantly of seeing their faces. I wanted to see the face of a child that you and I made. The faces of the two little babies that we *did make* but couldn't keep."

When Russell spoke next, his voice faltered. "I think you got to do that, babe. I think you saw our little angels, and that is exactly what they are: angels." He pulled Shasta close again, and their tears flowed freely with the cleansing power of a Christmas miracle created by two of the tiniest of Christmas angels.

"There was always one thing that confused me. There were four empty oatmeal cookie wrappers in the car when you were rescued, and I know you don't like them." He tilted his head and raised he eyebrows.

Shasta smiled and patted his face. "You'll be happy to know both your girls love oatmeal cookies, just like their dad."

Snow Days

Dalton:

Mrs. Davis looked out the kitchen window at their snow-covered neighborhood. Beth Avery, the little girl who lived next door, was rolling a ball for a snowman.

Mrs. Davis turned her head toward the den, where her son was eating a bowl of cereal and watching TV. "Dalton, why don't you get dressed and go outside? Beth is making a snowman. I don't think she is going to be able to get that second ball on without help."

She turned back to the window, talking more to herself than her son. "I feel sorry for her. She and her dad always built a snowman together. They never missed a snowfall. This is the first snow we have had since he passed away. I am sure she misses him, poor thing."

Dalton moaned but got up and slowly made his way to the kitchen, where he plopped his empty bowl down on the table. "Geesh, Mom. I don't really know her. She's just a kid."

Mrs. Davis dropped her dish rag in the sink. "Well, that's a shame. She lives right next door, and you don't even know her! That's terrible. She is a very sweet young girl. But as far as being a kid, she is only two or three years younger than you, and she will eventually catch up. Be her friend now when she needs you." She reached for his empty bowl. "Besides, what are you doing right this minute anyway? You might actually enjoy yourself. God gave you this beautiful snow day that closed the school, and you are going to waste the whole thing doing nothing in this house?"

Dalton moaned again and turned to go upstairs. A few minutes later, he came down fully dressed in boots, bib, and toboggan. He gave his mom an eye roll in one last protest as he headed out the front door.

Mrs. Davis checked on them through the window over the next couple of hours. Dalton helped Beth build not one snowman, but three. They used up practically all the snow in the Averys' little front yard. Mrs. Avery brought them cookies and hot chocolate at one point, and they sat on the front porch talking and laughing. Mrs. Davis smiled and went about her chores.

When Dalton came in the house close to dusk, his mom met him in the hallway. "Well, how did the snowman turn out?"

Dalton shrugged as he unlaced his boots. "Good, I guess. Boy, she really likes snow. She gets all excited about it. I like it too, I guess, but mostly just because we get the day off from school."

"Well, we don't get much snow around here, so it is something to get excited about. One of God's most beautiful masterpieces."

Dalton started up the stairs and his mom called after him. "Don't get too involved in anything. Your dad will be home any minute and we'll have supper." She turned toward the kitchen and paused, looking toward her son. "And thank you, Dalton," she said with a smile. "That was nice of you."

Dalton turned around when he reached the top of the staircase and shrugged. "Yeah. It wasn't too bad. She is a nice kid. And crazy about snow." He twirled his finger beside his head and laughed.

And so, a friendship was born. Not only did Dalton and Beth build a snowman every rare snowfall they were given, but also became inseparable all the other days. Dalton even swapped bedrooms upstairs so his bedroom window lined up with Beth's and they could open the window on warm nights and talk to each other across the way.

Beth blossomed into a natural beauty with a kind personality that drew people to her. She was well liked by all her classmates but was not part of the 'in' crowd. She was everyone's personal cheerleader for whatever they were trying to accomplish but wasn't the type to be on the cheerleading squad. Playing volleyball was more to her liking, and of course everything her youth group at church was involved in. She had a heart for missions and helping people. Losing her dad at an early age and dealing with that loss gave her a passion for helping others.

By the time Dalton turned sixteen, he was finally starting to lose his boyhood chubbiness. His brown curls were still a hot mess, but he learned to keep them at bay with a shorter haircut. Dalton, like Beth, was very well-liked by his peers. He played in every sport offered at school and excelled in most just because of his sheer bulk.

In the girl department, however, he did not excel. Growing up chubby, he had always been seen as the chubby boy no matter how much taller and slimmer his frame became. That really didn't matter to Dalton…until the year Beth finally caught up and became a freshman at their high school.

On her first day of school that year, he met her at the bus and showed her around Campus, making a few introductions to his buddies. By lunchtime, however, Beth was thriving on her own. She had her group of friends, and Dalton noticed some of the older guys were already beginning to hover. He had never thought of Beth as a girlfriend, just a buddy. Now seeing other guys looking at her in that way made him uncomfortable.

The only thing that really kept the real vultures away from Beth was her reputation. She was a devout Christian, and all the guys knew it. She was never going to be the girl to hop in your back seat for a good time.

The first Friday night football game in October was also Homecoming for the high school, which meant the Homecoming dance would follow the game. Dalton was afraid to ask Beth to go with him to the dance, but he was terrified some other guy would. As it turned out, no one did, so they planned to meet up at the dance and then he would give her a ride home. It was casual, not a date.

After the game, Dalton changed out of his football uniform with lightning speed and ran out of the locker room toward the school cafeteria, where the dance would be held. He didn't want Beth to get involved with anyone else before he got there. A few strides into his jog up the hill to the cafeteria, he heard someone call his name and turned around. It was Beth. She had waited for him outside the locker room at the field. He couldn't believe it. He stopped and waited for Beth to catch up. "Hey. I figured you would already be in there shaking a tailfeather by now."

Beth punched him in the arm and smiled. "Shake my tailfeather? Yeah, that's right. You know I dance like an injured ostrich. I am saving the shame of being my dance partner for you!"

They sat a table with their friends and laughed, danced like ostriches, and talked about the football game. Toward the end of the night, a slow song began to play, and the DJ announced it would be the last slow song of the night, so the guys better make their move. A few couples left from their tables, and Dalton saw his buddy Nick making eyes at Beth. Dalton reached over and grabbed Beth's hand almost by reflex. She looked at him, a little surprised.

Dalton winked. "I know you can't shake your booty. Let's see if you can slow dance without smashing my toes."

She smiled, and they made their way out to the dance floor. As Dalton pulled her close, he could smell her hair and feel her breath on his neck. If his own heart hadn't been pounding so hard in his chest, he might have felt hers beating. They had both exchanged hugs before. Beth was a big hugger for any occasion. But this wasn't a casual hug. This was intimate.

When the dance was over, Dalton slid his arms from around her waist down to her hands and stood there for a second just looking at her and holding her hands. She didn't try to pull away. She returned his gaze without a word. When the next song—an upbeat one—began to play, others started dancing all around them, but they didn't move.

Dalton looked around and smiled. "Well, want to boogie down again or head home?"

"Let's just head home. This is probably the last song anyway."

They gathered their stuff and headed to the car. They made idle chitchat about the game and school on the way home, but it felt forced.

Dalton parked his car in his drive and walked Beth across the lawn to her front door. Just before she reached for the doorknob, Dalton gently pulled Beth into his arms and gave her a kiss. It was gentle and not rushed. When he stopped, he let his forehead rest against hers. "I'll see you tomorrow. OK?" Beth nodded. Dalton turned and jumped off the front porch and disappeared into the night.

And just like that, they went from being buddies to being a couple.

Dalton sat at his dorm room desk, tapping his pencil on his textbook. He had been hard at it since his last class at eleven that morning. When his phone pinged, he let out a sigh and reached for it. He smiled when he saw that it was Beth. "Hey, babe! Boy, am I glad to hear your voice."

"You must be studying."

"How'd you know?"

"That's the only time I get this much excitement when I call. Hang in there. You are on the short rows. Think about poor me. I will just be getting started next year in college. You better have pity on me then like I do for you now."

"You'll breeze right through your classes. You're a bookworm. I am just a worm. A lazy slug. I am so ready to be done with classes, books, and studying."

"Well," Beth said with a smile in her voice, "speaking of breezing right through, guess what blew through here last night." She punched a couple of buttons on her phone. "Check the pic I just sent."

Dalton pulled his phone away from his ear and pulled up the photo. There was Beth standing in her front yard with her arm around a snowman. "You got snow! Wow. Nice snowman. How did you get the middle ball up there? Didn't go find some hunky next-door neighbor to help you, did you?"

"No. You know you're the only person I play in the snow with. Had to use my noggin. Got a plank out of the garage and propped it up on the bottom snowball and just slid the middle ball up the plank. It took some pushing, but there's no way I could have picked the ball up." She sighed. "I sure missed you being here. It wasn't the same. Wasn't much of a snow either. I had to use every flake in the yard to make a presentable snowman."

"I hate that I wasn't there too. I am tired of us being apart. I am so ready for you to get here in the fall. It will make my last year bearable."

He heard Beth moving, and he imagined her falling back on her bed and closing her eyes. "Me too. I know it isn't smart to do it, but I do wish I could fast forward time. I am so ready to be getting on with my life. I want to be with you, and I want to start planning our wedding, house hunt, and find my killer dream job as a nurse, and start having kids and—"

Dalton leaned back in his chair. "Whoa, Miss Time Traveler. You might be skipping over some pretty awesome life events, wishing your life away like that." He sighed and closed his eyes. His voice was softer. "I know what you mean, though. Hang in there, babe, OK? When we are old and gray and sick of each other, we might daydream about a day apart."

"Never in a million years." She sighed. "I'll let you go. Hunker down and study hard. I can't be associated with a college dropout."

They both said their goodbyes and, as they always did, they said "I love you" at the exact same time.

Dalton tried to get back into his studies after talking to Beth, but he was studied out. So when his roommate Richard came in the room, he closed his books.

Richard took his shirt off and thumbed through his drawer for a replacement. "Hey. Heading over to Mike's for a while. Want to come?" When Dalton hesitated, he added, "Chicks, beer, and best of all, no studying!"

"Nah. You know I have a girlfriend, and I'm not big on drinking."

"Dude, it hasn't stopped you before. Besides, you need to sow your wild oats before that chick ties you down for life."

Dalton slumped back in his chair. "That's the whole problem. I feel guilty already about the stupid stuff I've done. If Beth knew, it would break her heart. And as far as being tied down for life with her, that is exactly what I want. If we were together now, everything would be fine. I am out of sync without her."

Richard threw one of Dalton's shirts at him. "Dude, that is pathetic."

Dalton stared at the shirt, rubbing it between his fingers and glancing back at his books. It was an easy choice, although a regrettable one. He would be going out with Richard.

Beth:

Beth was so excited after high school graduation. It was the first step toward everything she was looking forward to in life. Her summer flew by as she got ready to pack for college. And because Dalton hadn't come home that summer, she was even more antsy to go.

Her only hesitation was leaving her mom. She did feel guilty about that. It had been just the two of them since her dad had died, and she hated to leave her alone. Her mom had a full life what with working full time, plus church and other activities; but Beth would miss her, and she worried her mom would be lonely.

Move-in day was an explosion of emotions. Beth was elated to be with Dalton again. Mrs. Avery cried after Beth's room was set up and there was nothing left to unpack. She gave Dalton a hug. "I can leave her easier knowing you are here too." Dalton blushed and nodded when she released him.

As soon as Mrs. Avery drove off, Beth jumped in Dalton arms, wrapping her legs around his waist. "OK, big man on Campus, show me around. Show me everything!"

Beth soon realized that Dalton really was a big man on Campus. They had been together for so long that it had been a while since she had really stepped back to notice how attractive Dalton had become. His baby fat had disappeared, and his curly hair was like a movie star's. Everyone they passed seemed to know him. Beth almost felt a little intimidated by his popularity. But alone, Dalton was still her boy next door who had become her whole world. He was still her best friend and her rock.

It didn't take long for them to get into a rhythm. Attending football games, lunch on days their schedules allowed, and midnight coffee runs when they had studies. Still, there was a lot of time when they were apart, and some days it felt like they were still miles apart instead of on the same campus.

Dalton had taken on extra classes every semester and during the summer so that he would graduate in December instead of the spring. After that, things would be better. Their plan was for him to find a job close by so they could still see each other while she continued her classes. The first thing on Dalton's shopping list was an engagement ring. Beth had her wedding all planned in her head, but it didn't feel right to set things in stone until a ring was on her finger.

The night before Thanksgiving break, Beth met Dalton at his car. He was driving home for the weekend. Beth's mom was picking her up the next morning. Their family was gathering at her aunt's house for the holiday, so Beth wouldn't be going home. She gave Dalton one last hug. "It stinks that we won't be together for Thanksgiving."

"Yeah, I know. I have a lot to talk to Mom and Dad about though, so it's probably a good thing."

"Really? What kind of things?"

"You know, father-son stuff. Financial stuff. Things are getting real now, ya know."

"I'm ready for real." She gave him another kiss on the cheek. "Tell them I said hello and Happy Thanksgiving."

Dalton said he would, and with that he got in and drove off. Beth noticed a thoughtful look on his face as he drove away. She felt apprehensive, but also enjoyed a twinge of excitement. She knew Dalton was just as anxious as she was to be married. Maybe he was going to jump ahead and ask his parents for a loan so he could give her a ring for Christmas.

But after Thanksgiving, Beth noticed a change in Dalton. He was more secretive and serious. She thought she must be correct that he was getting ready to make his proposal move. Every encounter they had, she secretly expected it to be *the moment*. Dalton had always been a sly person, so Beth was expecting the unexpected, which really kept her on her toes. It was distracting her from her studies, and she was having trouble relaxing at night. Her imagination was working overtime.

Early December, after Dalton's last exam, he called Beth. She was just cooling down from a jog and answered, breathing hard. "Hey. Did you kill your final exam, or did it kill you?"

"Let's just say I feel as out of breath as you sound—and just as glad it's over." He paused to open his dorm room door. "Hey, I know you probably still have some studying to do, but can we grab a coffee later tonight?"

Beth plopped down on the steps. "Sure. That sounds great. Oh, and have you heard the weather forecast? We might have snow flurries tonight! I am so excited!" She snapped her fingers. "Hey, let's meet at that cute coffee shop on Hawley Street. They have the prettiest Christmas decorations on that street, and we can get a window seat."

"You and your snow. You know, you really should move to the North Pole."

"If that's where you are, then my life would be perfect."

"No one gets 'perfect,' Beth." Dalton sounded sad. He sighed. "See you at eight."

And then as always, they both said "I love you" simultaneously and hung up.

Beth couldn't concentrate the rest of the day. Her heart told her that tonight was going to be the night. Dalton had finished his final exam and would be packing up tomorrow. College was one and done for him. Beth had one more exam and then she would be heading home too.

She arrived at the coffee shop an hour early to make sure she could grab a prized window seat. It really was the most picturesque view. Hallmark couldn't have done a better job decorating this little corner of town. On her walk there, she had felt snow in the air. They were still saying that there was only a slim chance of flurries, but she felt it would happen and soon. She could feel it in her bones like arthritis in an old person's knee.

Dalton came in, and they ordered their hot drinks. They made small talk until the drinks arrived. Dalton seemed aloof and kept his hands in his pockets most of the time. Beth wondered if he was holding onto her ring box.

Dalton shifted, wrapping his hands around his cup. His head was down and he didn't meet her gaze when he began to speak. "Look, Beth. We need to talk. I need to talk."

Beth didn't know why, but her nerves took over. She began talking and couldn't stop. She was rattling on about the possibility of snow, Christmas plans, her last exam—anything and everything to keep him from saying the thing she suddenly dreaded.

Dalton slammed his hand down on the table. "Beth!"

Beth stopped talking, and they both glanced around the coffee shop. Dalton's outburst had caused a few customers to throw inquiring glances their way.

"Sorry. Look, I really need to talk to you." He nodded toward the window. "Let's go outside. I know it's cold, but I want us to be alone."

Beth nodded in silence. They got up with their cardboard coffee cups in hand and headed outside.

As they sat on the sidewalk bench, Beth looked around. This would be an even better place to propose. Down on one knee by the town Christmas tree. Her nerves plus the cold made her shiver.

What came out of Dalton's mouth next was the very last thing Beth would have ever expected. It took her a moment to realize what he was saying. He was admitting to bad choices, missing her, feeling lonely, being at the wrong place with the wrong people, and giving in to temptation.

Beth was lightheaded and fuzzy. For a few seconds, she was pretty sure she was floating above her body and couldn't hear the foreign words coming out of his mouth. But his last sentence would be embedded in her brain for eternity. With tears in his eyes, looking as ashamed and remorseful as if he were being sentenced to life in prison, he said, "And she's pregnant."

It was all Beth could do to just breathe. It felt like someone had peeled her skin back and poured a bucket of sand into her chest. Everything felt tight and ready to explode.

Dalton tried to reach over and take her hand, but Beth pulled back, dropping her coffee. Dalton reached down to pick it up and placed both their cups in the trash. When he sat back down, he slid closer to her on the bench. "Beth, I am so sorry. I don't know what to say. I have been over this conversation in my head a million times. It made me sick every time. I messed up. I messed up royally. But to make you pay for something that I did... It is killing me. It has been killing me for weeks thinking about it."

"So, what are you saying?"

Dalton slumped back on the bench. "I talked to my parents about it over Thanksgiving, and my dad wouldn't hear of any solution other than me being a man and doing the right thing by her and the baby. He is insisting that I marry her."

"No. What about me, Dalton? I can't believe your dad would suggest that. He knows how much we love each other. What about *me?*"

"Remember the day last year when we were wishing you could speed time up? Well, I would give anything, anything at all, to go back in time now. I would go back and stop myself from being stupid." He slumped back on the bench. "You know what the worst part of dealing with it was? I couldn't even talk to my best friend about it. *You.*" He stood and reached for Beth's hand. "Come on. Let me walk you back to your dorm. It's cold out here. I can see you are shivering."

Beth allowed him to pull her to her feet and wrap his arms around her.

Dalton rubbed her back and whispered in her ear. "I am so sorry, Beth. Please don't hate me. You probably should. But please don't."

Beth buried her face in his chest, breathing in his scent. "So, this is it for us, then."

"I don't have a choice, Beth. I have to do what's right." He slipped his arms down and took Beth's hands. "Come on. Let me walk you back."

Beth pulled her hands away and folded them across her chest. "No. I just want to sit here for a little bit. Please just go." Beth wasn't even sure her legs would work. She felt shaky. She sat back down on the bench.

He started to argue but with tears in her eyes she held her hand up in protest. "No. You just need to go."

Dalton nodded and put his hands in his pockets. He turned and made several strides down the path before he turned. "Beth." She looked toward him. "I do love you. I will always love you. Please remember that."

Beth could see his silhouette against the lamppost light. and as he turned to leave, she realized that it had begun to snow. Big fat beautiful snowflakes drifted down as she watched him walk away.

Beth didn't tell anyone about the breakup. She didn't allow herself to believe it yet. She held out hope that it was all a dream, or that Dalton would change his mind. She prayed that while he was home for Christmas, he would convince his parents there was another solution. One that included Beth, like they had always planned.

But Dalton didn't come home for Christmas. She later learned that he had gone home with *her*. She wanted him there when she told her parents. His new life was emerging, and Beth's was dying.

Beth finally told her mom on Christmas Day. Mrs. Avery demanded to know why Dalton wasn't there and why Beth was so sullen. When Beth told her, they sat on the couch and cried together. *A Christmas Story* played on TV. She had no idea how many times it played through while the tears flowed.

The next morning when Beth came downstairs, she noticed her mom had removed Dalton's present from under the tree. She had not even told Beth what she had purchased, and now she didn't care. Later that day, Beth and her mom decided to take down the Christmas decorations. Beth needed to be busy doing something, and the decorations brought sadness instead of joy. It was the earliest they had ever removed them.

That evening, they closed the blinds so the other twinkling lights in the neighborhood were hidden from view.

Beth saw Dalton only once after the night he chiseled away part of her heart. It was the following summer. She was sitting on her front porch when Dalton pulled up in his parents' drive.

He hopped out, went straight to the passenger's rear door, and leaned in. He came out with a baby carrier. Little yellow booties kicked at a pink coverlet. A girl. Dalton had a daughter. The baby's mom came around to his side of the car and he handed the carrier off to her, but only after a couple of tummy tickles.

Dalton's parents practically ran out to meet them. They all looked so excited. The little bundle of pink and yellow made them all so happy and yet it had taken away all of Beth's joy.

Beth noticed that Dalton's wife didn't look all that much different from herself. Same hair, eyes, and frame. The biggest difference was that she glowed. Maybe it was leftover pregnancy glow she had heard so much about, or maybe it was her imagination. After all, she was where Beth wanted to be.

As the Davis family began to head inside, Dalton went to the back of the car. He was getting out luggage when he looked over at the Avery house. He saw Beth on the porch. His face lit up, and he threw his hand up in a wave…but stopped short. Beth met his gaze but did not return his smile. She stared long enough to see his smile fade. Then she got up and walked inside. Not much of a triumph, but life was not business as usual for her anymore.

Beth cut her visit home short and left later that night. She didn't want to take any chances of seeing any more happy family moments. She should have been glad Dalton looked happy and that his mistake had still led to a happy ending. She was not.

Beth's college years didn't fly by in a blur. Every single moment of every day was a painful exercise in getting out of there as quickly as possible. She didn't know what was next for her, but she wanted to get off the campus where her world had ended. She avoided Hawley Street whenever possible, sometimes walking thirty minutes out of her way to go around it.

It turned out that what was next for her was watching her mother slip away. Her first nursing job would be taking care of her mother through her last days of colon cancer. She was grateful for the timing, if there could be anything to be grateful for in death. Her mother had been diagnosed a couple of months before Graduation but hadn't told Beth. When she moved home afterwards, it was as if her mom had given herself permission to give in to the disease.

It was peaceful, and Beth got to be there through every moment. They laughed. They cried and reminisced. Toward the end, Beth's mom talked for hours about Beth's father. It had been so many years that much of what she retold Beth had forgotten. It was a nice gift. In her last few hours, Beth heard her talking *to* her father. She told him how proud she was of Beth and how well she had tried to take care of her. Tears streamed down Beth's face. She wished she could see and talk to her dad as well.

Beth stayed home after the funeral to settle all her mother's affairs and to apply for jobs. She accepted a nursing job in a hospital in another town, and her aunt and uncle volunteered to help her sell the house. Beth knew she couldn't come back here. Her mother's passing had been a beautiful time, and she was leaving with that on her heart.

Plus she couldn't see herself living next door to Dalton's parents. That was too much. So, she loaded up all the things she wanted to keep and left the rest behind. All the memories sealed up and packed away.

Beth thrived at her work. She found solace in helping patients. She was well liked by all the staff and was always the first to volunteer for undesirable shifts or tasks. It was common knowledge that she would cover any shift if someone needed to swap out. She didn't have kids or a husband, or even a boyfriend, so she used that as her reasoning for being available to work the holidays. "You'll pay me back later when I have six kids and workaholic husband," she would joke. In her heart, which was still extremely tender and scared, she didn't see that happening. Her job was her family now.

With the male hospital staff, she had another reputation: untouchable. She turned down most offers for dates. Occasionally, just to prove she wasn't a prude, she would accept one, but she never agreed to a second. She gave all her affection to her patients, and she told herself it was working well for everyone. She was damaged goods. Men would be better off not attempting to *fix* her.

In late January, there was a terrible ice storm. The roads were a nightmare and the city practically shut down. Nurses and doctors on duty were asked to stay the night. It was too dangerous for the next shift to try to make the drive in. It was standard procedure and something Beth always volunteered to do, even if she wasn't on call when the storm hit. She didn't mind.

But she could never sleep in the hospital. It wasn't where she slept—it was where she worked, and she couldn't separate the two.

So, on this stormy night, instead of trying to fight it, she headed to the break room for a cup of coffee. One of the day shift nurses had some fancy creamers for the people who got stuck working the graveyard, and Beth fixed herself a large cup. She slumped in a chair, propped her feet on one of the tables, and let out a sigh after her first sip.

Dr. Hamilton came in and headed to the coffee pot. "Making yourself at home, I see."

Most nurses would have popped up and been embarrassed at having been caught in that way. Beth shrugged and kept her position. She knew Dr. Hamilton from the few patients they had worked with together. He was a nice guy. He was single but had never asked her out. She liked that about him. Maybe he had a girlfriend. She didn't know, but she never felt threatened by him. Maybe it was his looks. Tall, lanky, large Adam's apple, glasses, and bright orange hair. It was rumored he'd been called Big Bird in college. He played basketball, so the Larry Byrd connection was part of the equation, along with his goofy looks.

In terms of new patients coming in, it looked like it was going to be a slow night. But no one would ever say that. It was a well-known jinx in the ER.

Dr. Hamilton took the seat at the table facing Beth. They chitchatted about different patients and things going on in the hospital. After a few minutes, he left to go check on a patient.

When he returned, he looked excited. "Hey, Beth, come look. The sleet has changed to snow. Boy, it's really coming down." He nodded toward the window at the end of the hall. "Come on."

Beth didn't move. "No thanks. I am not really a snow person."

Dr. Hamilton looked dumbfounded. "How could you not be a snow person? It's beautiful. Maybe dangerous to travel in but come look at these big fluffy flakes float down outside and tell me you don't see the beauty in it."

When Beth still didn't budge, he made his way back to his seat. He looked at her intently. "I've heard about you. You volunteer for all the crappy hours, working through storms like tonight, and even working Christmas Day. So, I guess you don't like Christmas either? The most wonderful time of the year?"

Beth shrugged.

Dr. Hamilton set his cup down on the table and folded his arms. "OK, spill, Beth. Tell me your story. Nobody does these kinds of things without a reason. You're a loving person. I've seen it with the patients. But something tells me you have had a lot of heartbreak. Spill."

"Look, Dr. Hamilton—"

Dr. Hamilton held up his hand. "Everyone calls me Robbie."

Beth sighed. "Robbie. As much as I would just *love* to pour my heart out to someone, I barely know—"

"How can you say that?" Robbie interrupted. "We are on first-name terms now. You know me." He leaned forward, putting his elbows on the table. "Tell ya what. Let's let fate decide. We could have a long boring night sitting here staring at each other, or all hell could break lose in the next five minutes. Start your story. Talk until we get called. Let's see how far you get."

She hesitated.

"It'll be just between us. Your secret will be safe with me."

So, for whatever reason, Beth began to tell her tale. Every tear-filled moment of her life, from the passing of her father to Dalton, to her mother's last days. When she was done, she felt extremely tired. It had all been built up for so long. It felt good to get it all out to at least one person. But now she was spent. Robbie had not interrupted her a single time. He'd never asked any questions. He'd just let her tell as much or as little as she wanted to share.

When she was done, she stood up. "Well, that is my sad story. So if you don't mind, I think the show is over and I am going to try and go sleep." She turned toward the door.

"Wow."

She turned to look at him. "What?"

He looked up at her and said it louder: "Wow, Beth. Just wow. I don't even know how to respond to all that."

Beth shrugged and headed out the door. "Neither do I, Robbie. Neither do I."

After that night, she and Robbie became friends. They didn't date, and Beth was grateful he never asked. What she really needed was a friend. They never went out after work or called each other. But if they were ever in the cafeteria at the same time, they always sat together. They exchanged jokes in passing, and if they met in the break room for coffee, they would linger to chat. They were the two staples for holiday shifts and storm coverage.

It was nice. Beth had always made her friends play second fiddle to Dalton. She didn't know how to be best friends with a female. But Robbie was comfortable to her. He was helping her heal.

One day, Beth was standing at the nurse's station on the third floor making final notes at the end of her shift when Robbie came running down the hall. Beth looked up. Her smile disappeared at the look on his face. He pulled her down the hall a few steps. "Robbie. What is it? What's wrong?"

Robbie gently reached for Beth's hands and looked into her eyes. "Beth, I'm sorry and maybe I shouldn't tell you. Maybe you don't even want to know."

Beth stiffened. "Know what, Robbie? Just tell me."

"It's Dalton, Beth. He's here. He is a patient of Dr. Thomas's."

Beth pulled back. "Dalton? My Dalton? He's...Dr. Thomas's?"

Robbie nodded. "Yeah. Dalton Davis. That's right, isn't it? I'm sorry, Beth. It's not good. He doesn't have much time."

Beth put her hand to her mouth and tears formed in her eyes. "I can't believe it. I—" She stopped in mid-sentence, not sure what to say. Not even sure of what to think.

Robbie put his hand on Beth's shoulder. "They are moving him into Room 402. His family is in with Dr. Thomas going over a few things, and I heard them say they were going to the cafeteria to take a break before they go back in to be with him when..." He paused. "Just to be with him. If you want to go see him, now would be the time."

Beth nodded and ran toward the stairs. She took them two at a time, and was out of breath by the time she reached Dalton's room. She peeked in first to make sure he was alone. When she saw that he was, she held her breath and walked to the far side of his bed.

He must have heard movement because he opened his eyes, and then he smiled. "Beth. I was praying you would come. I can't believe you are here." He reached toward her, and she took hold of his hand. He felt so weak.

Beth gave Dalton a smile, trying to keep her emotions in check. "Hey. How are you doing?"

Dalton gave her a weak smile. "I'm good. It turns out that dying is the easiest thing I have ever done. I just lay here and do nothing, and it just happens. Slowly, as it turns out, but it happens all by itself."

Dalton rubbed his thumb back and forth across Beth's hand. "Beth Avery, the love of my life. I can't believe you are really here. Do you work here? In this hospital? I always wondered where you were."

Tears flowed freely now down Beth's face. She nodded. Trying to compose herself, she tried to lighten things up. "Took the second job that was offered to me. No regrets. It's a good hospital. You are in a good place."

Dalton raised his eyebrows. "Oh, yeah. But…the second offer? What was the first?"

Beth smiled and wiped her eyes. "Funny story, actually. My first job interview was at an abortion clinic."

Dalton gasped. "No way, Beth."

Beth laughed. "Mom had just died. I saw the ad and I thought, 'Yeah. I have been wrong about this. These young girls should get rid of their unplanned babies. These babies are ruining a lot of lives. Not just the parents, but innocent bystanders just like me."

"I am not believing what I am hearing."

"Oh, here is where it gets good. Halfway through the interview, the manager was showing me around the facility, and I saw the most misleading poster of an aborted baby, and I went off. I yelled and tore the poster down. I called them all liars and baby killers and started spouting Bible verses."

"Now, that's my Beth."

"The security guard escorted me out and they issued a restraining order to keep me off the property. I heard they put up my picture at the front desk in case I returned."

They both laughed. Really laughed. It felt good.

He held her hand tighter. "Beth, I am so sorry about your mom. I wanted to go to the funeral, but my parents didn't let me know until it was too late. I guess they didn't think it was a good idea. By the time I found out and came home, your uncle was having the estate sale and you were gone."

All Beth could do was nod.

Dalton tugged on her hand. "Hey, remember the year we tied those cables across the yard from your bedroom window to mine and hung out that Santa's sleigh between our houses?"

Beth laughed. "Yes. We almost tore up both our window frames. My mom was so mad, but she didn't make us take it down." Smiling, she continued. "Of course, she also didn't let us string it up any more after that year."

"I bought it."

"What? Bought what?"

"The Santa's sleigh. It was part of the estate sale. My daughter walked over with me that day and had a fit when she saw it. Had to have it. It goes in our front yard every year. I couldn't believe you didn't want to keep it."

Beth shrugged. "Christmas sort of lost a lot of its joy for me."

"No way, Beth. What about snow? I know there's no way that could ever fade."

Beth looked down and shook her head. When she looked back up and met his eyes, she could tell he knew why.

"It snowed that night."

Beth nodded. "You didn't just break my heart, Dalton. You shredded it."

"I know. I know, because I broke my own. Beth, life changed for me too. Every joy since that night has been clouded. I never forgot you. You really were the love of my life, Beth. I have thought of you every day since that terrible night I walked away. I was stupid enough to think if I just contacted you that we could still at least be friends again. We could talk, like we used to, and things would be better. But I knew that was selfish. I still just needed you. I needed you as my friend if I couldn't have anything else." He sighed. "I have lived with regret and second guesses. But then there is my little girl. Oh, Beth she is the best thing ever, and I am going to miss so much." Tears were rolling down Dalton's face now as well. "Maybe that is the price God is making me pay. She took me away from you, and now He is taking me away from her."

Beth shook her head. "God doesn't work like that."

"Beth, do you have kids? Are you married?"

Beth shook her head.

"Don't do that. Don't give up on life because of me. Get married. Have kids. Find your Christmas joy. And for heaven's sake, don't forget your love of snow." He smiled. "I mean, come on. How many snowmen have you disappointed?"

"I'll try. No promises, but I'll try."

A child's chatter could be heard down the hall. Dalton smiled. "That would be my little Claire coming. I am glad you will get to see her."

Beth stroked Dalton's cheek. "I should go now." She reached down to kiss Dalton on the cheek, and she whispered in his ear. "I never stopped loving you."

He lifted his hand to Beth's cheek, his expression concerned. "I don't have long, Beth. I think today's the day. When I see God, I am going to ask Him to let it snow for you. I want you to get your joy back."

Beth smiled. "Dalton, you do know it's seventy-five degrees outside, right?"

"You do know He's God, right?"

Dalton's family came into the room. Beth pretended to be tucking in his blankets. She stole one last look at Dalton. He had closed his eyes. Beth kept her head down when she slipped out. She didn't want his mom to recognize her.

Her eyes connected with Claire's right before she left the room. The little girl smiled at her, and she could see Dalton in the child's face. A little piece of him would still be here. It was a sad but nice thought.

Robbie was getting off the elevator as Beth rounded the corner. When she saw him, she fell into his arms. Robbie rubbed her back. "Did you get to see him?"

Beth nodded.

"I talked to Dr. Thomas," he said. "He is going to keep me updated. He will let me know as soon as... well, as soon as he's gone."

Beth nodded and pulled back, wiping tears from her face. "Thank you for telling me. I am so glad we got to talk one last time."

Robbie looked perplexed. "Talk? Beth, Dalton is—"

"I've got to get out of here. I'll be outside." Beth looked back down the hall toward Dalton's room. "Thanks again." She wiped her running nose. "Please find me. OK?"

Robbie nodded and Beth walked away.

Robbie continued to remain close to Dalton's room. Keeping watch when he could, as he'd promised. When he saw Dr. Thomas coming down the hall, he approached him. "Hey, thanks again for giving Beth a window to see Mr. Davis. Question, though: you said he was nonresponsive, right?"

Dr. Thomas nodded. "Yes. Has been for days. Family just finalized the decision to stop all measures. Waiting on one more family member to arrive and then—" He looked up when he saw a couple walking toward Dalton's room. He nodded in that direction. "That should be them." He turned to Robbie and placed his hand on his back. "I'll come find you after."

Robbie nodded.

Thirty minutes later, Robbie found Beth standing outside in the Serenity Park area. This was a tree-lined quiet area for families to get away from the hospital.

When she felt Robbie's hand on her shoulder, she knew Dalton was gone. She turned around and buried her head in his chest.

Robbie wrapped his arms around her and gently rubbed her back. "I'm sorry, Beth."

Beth cried for several minutes. She cried like she hadn't cried in years. All the pent-up sadness came pouring out. When she finally pulled away, Robbie handed her a tissue. With her head down, she blew her nose and wiped her eyes. Through blurry eyes, she saw white covering the ground. She looked up and the sky was covered in white, floating down to the ground. Beth gasped. "Snow!"

Robbie looked around. The park area was surrounded by Bradford pear trees that were at their peak with heavy blooms. The breeze had kicked up, and the air was full of swirling white blossoms falling like snow. It was the most blooms he had ever seen. The ground was quickly covered like a winter's dusting of snow. "Yeah, it does look like snow."

Beth smiled. "Dalton said the first thing he was going to do was to ask God to make it snow for me." She laughed and held out her arms catching the blooms. "He did it. He made it snow just for me. He made it snow."

Christmas Shorts

Keith walked into gift wrap mayhem. Wrapping paper, gift boxes and tissue paper covered the dining room table.

Ruth gasped. "Oh, my goodness. I had no idea what time it was. I have got to clear this stuff up before the kids get home."

Keith looked at the wrapped gifts. "Geesh, all this for the kids?"

"No. Some of it is for the needy family we got from the angel tree at church." She held up her finger. "But I used the same wrapping paper, so I have to get rid of the evidence."

Keith pulled out a chair and sat down. "I told you, babe, that ship has sailed. Josh is a smart kid. He has this stuff already figured out."

Ruth frowned. "Don't say that. I mean, yes, he is smart and is asking a lot of questions, but I want just one more year of magic." She sighed. "The last year with your baby is the sweetest one, I think." She thrust a stack of gifts at Keith. "Go put these in the trunk of your car. The kids won't look in there. I still have a couple more things to buy before we drop them off." She began clearing the table. "I can't leave one scrap of wrapping paper on the floor."

Keith hesitated before going out. "By the way, what's for supper tonight? I am starving already."

"Food court. Tonight, we have that chorale thing at the mall. Josh is singing." She snapped her fingers. "Plus, he can see Santa. It will probably be our only chance. That Santa is such a good one too. He is so sweet with the kids, and his beard is the real deal."

"I'm telling you—"

Ruth slapped his arm. "Not another word. Go!" She shooed him toward the door. "No ships are sailing around here until I pull up the anchor."

That night at the mall, the family had a rushed but nice evening. They all got their favorites at the food court, and the choir sang like little angels, which the crowds seemed to enjoy, and that pleased the choir director.

After they ate, Sam slipped away to hang out in the video store with some friends. Ruth and Keith took Josh to see Santa. As they stood in line and tried to make small talk with Josh about what he would say to Santa, he wasn't very forthcoming.

Lists had been made weeks ago, so there were no secrets there. It was a family rule to ask for only three gifts from Santa. The kids received so much from family and friends that limits had to be made.

When it was Josh's turn, he timidly walked up to Santa, eyeing him closely.

Santa picked him up and plopped him on his lap. "Well, young man. I heard your choir group singing earlier. It was simply beautiful."

Ruth smiled and nudged Keith. "That's a good start. Told you this Santa was the best. He noticed Josh in the choir."

Keith rolled his eyes but made no comment.

Josh and Santa went through the usual ritual of small talk and the delivery of a complimentary candy cane. Santa placed Josh back down to his feet and nodded a quick goodbye. Josh made it only a couple steps before he abruptly stopped. He made eye contact with Ruth and then ran back to Santa. The big man leaned down toward the child and Josh covered his mouth and whispered something in Santa's ear. When Josh turned back around, he had a sheepish grin on his face. Santa didn't skip a beat and was on to his next visitor.

Ruth grabbed Keith's arm. "Wait a minute. What do you think he said? What just happened? He has asked for something special, and now we are screwed."

Keith shrugged. "Who knows? He for sure isn't going to tell you. Besides, I told you, Josh is too smart for this. You are trying to keep him a baby, and he isn't."

Keith was right. Over the next couple of days, no amount of prodding could make Josh give up even a hint as to what his exchange with Santa had been.

Ruth wouldn't give up though. Christmas was still a week away. There was time.

Christmas Eve fell on a Saturday, so Keith didn't have to work. He was awakened by the sound of rattling paper at six in the morning. He squinted open one eye lid to see Ruth wrapping presents on the floor of their bedroom. Same wrapping paper as last week. "Babe, it is six a.m. What in the world are you doing?"

Ruth blew a stray hair from her face. "I know. Sorry. I couldn't sleep. I had one more gift to wrap for the angel tree family, which by the way I need you to deliver this morning. The families are coming to the church by one to pick them up. And-" Ruth tapped her temple, "I got one more gift for Josh." She waved her finger at him. "Now don't say anything. I know we already have his three. But I used my own stash to buy him something special. I am pretty sure my CSI skills figured out what he asked Santa for, and I can't wait to see his face tomorrow morning."

Keith grunted and threw back the covers.

An hour later and with his second cup of coffee in hand, Keith went into the bedroom to retrieve the last gift to take to the church. Ruth was in the bathroom brushing her teeth. She looked over at him through the doorway. She heard noises from upstairs signaling the kids were up and about. She ran to the bed, toothbrush hanging out of her mouth. She thrust one package in Keith's hand and ran to the closet with the other one. She shooed Keith away with her hand. "Hurry, go drop those off, and when you get back, we'll do pancakes."

Keith pulled up to the church, parking beside a beat-up Toyota he didn't recognize. A teenage boy sat in the passenger side of the car. He glanced at Keith as he got out of the car but didn't return his greeting. Instead, he just stared down at the floor, ignoring him completely.

Ms. Reynolds, the chairperson of the angel tree committee, came out the door, talking and walking alongside an older woman. Ms. Reynolds looked relieved to see Keith and was animated as she approached him. "Keith, just in time. I just called Ruth and she said you were on your way." She motioned toward the older lady. "This is Ms. Austin. Ruth had her angel, so the gifts are for her.

Ms. Austin had to come early because she has to go into work later today, so we can just put the gifts straight into her vehicle."

Keith nodded and popped the trunk. He transferred the gifts into Ms. Austin's car and nodded toward the teenager in the front seat. "I hope my wife got him exactly what he wanted."

The older lady puffed. "I don't care a thing in the world about what he wants. I am just trying to get that boy what he needs. Mama died, Daddy's run off, and I am just doing the best I can." She slammed the trunk lid and nodded. "He's a good kid, though, and I sure do appreciate what y'all doing here. You a true blessing." She made her way back to the driver's door and crawled in.

Ms. Austin backed out of her parking space, as her grandson smirked. "I bet I got some more of that Walmart Great Value garbage that they wouldn't dare make their kids wear."

Ms. Austin shot him a sideways smile. "You better hope you did. You are growing like a weed, so it's that or go to school naked or in some of your grandma's clothes." She smiled. "Come to think of it, you might look kind of cute in my blue pantsuit." She slapped him on the thigh, and he finally returned her smile.

Christmas morning was chaos as usual. Josh and Sam were up at daybreak. They waited anxiously, eyeing all the gifts under the tree. Family tradition dictated that they had to sit patiently until Keith had a cup of coffee in hand and Ruth had arranged the gifts.

She had her own pecking order to the gift opening. The last gift was always the best one, so that the anticipation built with each gift. Each boy took his turn opening his gifts and seemed pleased with Santa's choices.

When their traditional three gifts were all opened, talk turned toward breakfast. Ruth held her hand up. "Wait; there is one more special gift this year that Santa left for Josh."

Sam sat up and raised his eyebrows. "Hey, he got his three already."

Ruth shrugged. "I know, but this year he left something extra." She turned to Josh. "Maybe something special he asked Santa for."

She handed the last package over to Josh, and he excitedly tore into the paper. Ruth shifted back to sit beside Keith on the floor and watched, excitement visible on her own face.

When Josh finished ripping the last of the paper off and opened the white box, he looked ecstatic, but Ruth's excitement disappeared. She sat with her mouth hanging open in confusion. Josh pulled out a pair of red athletic shorts with a green moose emblem on the waistband. He held them up to his own waist, and they were obviously too big for him. He looked up at Ruth with complete shock on his face. "I don't believe it. He got them. Santa got me Christmas shorts!"

Keith looked over at Ruth and whispered. "Is that what your CSI skills advised you to buy?"

Ruth turned to Keith. "Oh, no. I mixed up the packages. You took his gift to the church."

But Josh was dancing around. "I don't believe it. I told Santa to get me a pair of Christmas shorts, and he did it. He really did it. Nobody knew that's what I asked for. Nobody!"

Sam smirked. "Why did you ask for shorts, Josh? It's the dead of winter, and dude, those are way too big for you. I think the jolly old elf made a mistake."

Josh was still dancing around with the biggest grin on his face. "I don't know. Shorts just popped in my head. I didn't tell him what size. But he did it. He brought me what I asked for, and nobody else knew. Nobody!"

Keith patted Ruth on the thigh and whispered in her ear. "Well, I would say it all worked out. Looks like a Christmas miracle to me, babe. So, I guess you got your one more year of magic, after all."

Ruth nodded, tears in her eyes, as she watched Josh stare at his oversized, gaudy green shorts and hug them to his chest.

Later that morning, Keith was getting his second cup of coffee and Ruth was cramming wrapping paper in the trash can. "Hey," he said, "by the way, what was the gift that wound up going to the church family?"

Ruth pushed her hair back and shrugged. "Oh, nothing special. I was wrong anyway, plus we got our Christmas miracle, and that's all that matters."

Meanwhile, that Christmas morning across town in the Austin home, one pessimistic teenage boy had his faith in generosity and the human spirit rekindled as he opened the $300 iPad, he'd wished for instead of a pair of green Christmas shorts.

CPSIA information can be obtained
at www.ICGtesting.com
Printed in the USA
LVHW040740201222
735517LV00008B/769

9 798885 312547